Scarface Claw

Lynley Dodd

PUFFIN

WHO
is the roughest
and toughest
of cats?
The boldest,
the bravest,
the fiercest of cats?
Wicked of eye
and fiendish of paw
is mighty,
magnificent,
SCARFACE CLAW.

Scaredy cats tremble
and people all shout,
whenever this tomcat
is out and about.
No matter what happens,
whoever might call,
there's NOTHING
that frightens him,
nothing at all.

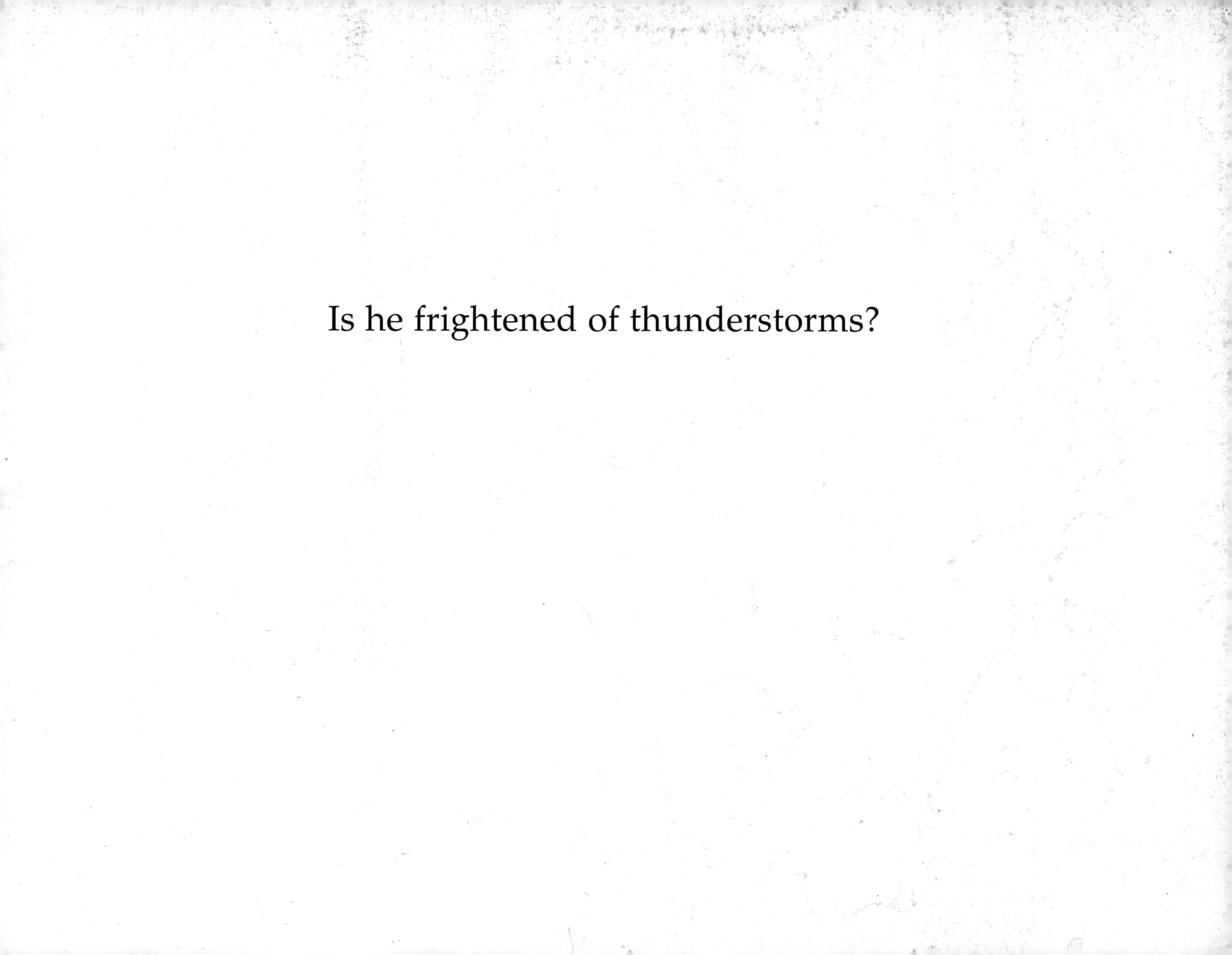

Is he frightened of thunderstorms?

Certainly not.

Is he scared of the dark?

Not a jittery jot.

Is he frightened of dogs
when they lollop and leap?

He washes his whiskers
and goes back to sleep.

-oo-ee-oo-ee-oo-ee-oo-ee-
EASTERN FIRE SERVICE

Does he jump at the sound
of a fire engine wail?

oo-ee-oo-ee-
e-oo-ee-

He pretends not to hear it
and chases his tail.

Is he frightened of spiders
all hairy and black?

He bustles them
out of their corners
and back.

GRO

No matter what happens,
whoever might call,
there's NOTHING
that frightens him,
nothing at all . . .

except . . .

the wickedest tomcat
that ever you saw,
the mighty,
magnificent,
SCARFACE CLAW.

PUFFIN BOOKS
Published by the Penguin Group: London, New York, Australia,
Canada, India, Ireland, New Zealand and South Africa
Penguin Books Ltd, Registered Offices:
80 Strand, London WC2R 0RL, England

puffinbooks.com

First published in New Zealand by Mallinson Rendel Publishers Limited 2001
Published in Puffin Books 2002
Published in this edition 2003
Reissued in 2009
029

Made and Printed in China
ISBN: 978-0-140-56886-8